P9-APB-689

Let's Compare, if You Dare!

Tracy Kompelien

Consulting Editors, Diane Craig, M.A./Reading Specialist
and Susan Kosel, M.A. Education

ABDO
Publishing Company

Published by ABDO Publishing Company, 4940 Viking Drive, Edina, Minnesota 55435.

Copyright © 2007 by Abdo Consulting Group, Inc. International copyrights reserved in all countries.
No part of this book may be reproduced in any form without written permission from the publisher.
SandCastle™ is a trademark and logo of ABDO Publishing Company.

Printed in the United States.

Credits
Edited by: Pam Price
Curriculum Coordinator: Nancy Tuminelly
Cover and Interior Design and Production: Mighty Media
Photo Credits: Brand X Pictures, Photodisc, ShutterStock, Wewerka Photography

Library of Congress Cataloging-in-Publication Data

Kompelien, Tracy, 1975-
     Let's compare, if you dare! / Tracy Kompelien.
       p. cm. -- (Math made fun)
     ISBN 10 1-59928-537-1 (hardcover)
     ISBN 10 1-59928-538-X (paperback)

     ISBN 13 978-1-59928-537-5 (hardcover)
     ISBN 13 978-1-59928-538-2 (paperback)
     1. Size perception--Juvenile literature. 2. Size judgment--Juvenile literature. I. Title.

BF299.S5K66 2006
152.14'2--dc22

                                                                   2006021564

SandCastle Level: Transitional

SandCastle™ books are created by a professional team of educators, reading specialists, and content developers around five essential components—phonemic awareness, phonics, vocabulary, text comprehension, and fluency—to assist young readers as they develop reading skills and strategies and increase their general knowledge. All books are written, reviewed, and leveled for guided reading, early reading intervention, and Accelerated Reader® programs for use in shared, guided, and independent reading and writing activities to support a balanced approach to literacy instruction. The SandCastle™ series has four levels that correspond to early literacy development. The levels help teachers and parents select appropriate books for young readers.

Emerging Readers
(no flags)

Beginning Readers
(1 flag)

Transitional Readers
(2 flags)

Fluent Readers
(3 flags)

These levels are meant only as a guide. All levels are subject to change.

To compare

is to find how things
are different or alike.

Words used to
describe comparing:

bigger	**less than**
equal to	**same**
greater than	**smaller**

1 2 3 4 5 6 7 8 9 10

4 is greater than **3.**

4 are greater

than **3** .

Greater than can also be written using the > symbol.

4 > 3

1 2 3 4 5 6 7 8 9 10

1 is less than **2.**

1 🏍️ is less than

2 🏍️🏍️ .

Less than can also
be written using
the < symbol.
1 < 2

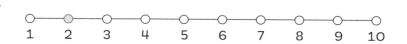

1 2 3 4 5 6 7 8 9 10

2 is equal to **2.**

2 **is** equal to **2** .

Equal to can also
be written using
the = symbol.
2 = 2

A  is

bigger than a 🍓.

I can also say that the size of the banana is greater than the size of the strawberry.

The  is smaller than the .

I can also say that the size of the blueberry is less than the size of the cherry.

This red

and this green

are the same size.

I can also say that the size of the red apple is equal to the size of the green apple.

Let's Compare, if You Dare!

Jim thinks he can throw a greater distance than Cher.
Cher says, "Let's throw and then compare!"

twelve
12

Jim throws first and almost hits the wall. Cher's ball lands right next to Jim's ball.

fourteen
14

Jim says,
"Isn't that fine!
Your distance is
equal to mine!"

Compare Every Day!

The truck is bigger than the car.

The puppy is smaller than the dog.

twenty
20

The pineapple is bigger than the orange.

Can you compare the plants?

Both plants come up to my knees, so I know they are of equal size.

Glossary

alike – almost the same.

different – not the same.

distance – the amount of space between two places.

symbol – an object that represents something else.